New Moon

SPORTS

What Sports Can Do for You
and What You Can Do with Sports

The New Moon Books Girls Editorial Board

Flynn Berry · Lauren Calhoun · Ashley Cofell

Morgan Fykes · Katie Hedberg · Elizabeth Larsson

Priscilla Mendoza · Julia Peters-Axtell · Caitlin Stern

CROWN PUBLISHERS, INC. ♛ NEW YORK

For every girl who has been inspired by the energy of sports

Text copyright © 1999 by New Moon Publishing, Inc.

Material on page 40 by Diane DeGennaro originally appeared in *New Moon* magazine.

Published by Crown Publishers, Inc., a Random House company, 201 East 50th Street, New York, New York 10022.

CROWN and colophon are trademarks of Random House, Inc.

www.randomhouse.com/kids

Printed in the United States of America
August 1999

Library of Congress Cataloging-in-Publication Data
New moon. Sports / the New moon books girls editorial board. —1st ed.
p. cm.
Includes bibliographical references.
Summary: Examines the role of sports in girls' lives, including the history of women in sports, famous women athletes, great sports for girls, and ways to get involved in athletics.
ISBN 0-517-88583-2 (trade pbk.) — ISBN 0-517-88584-0 (lib. bdg.)
1. Sports for women—Juvenile literature. [1. Sports for women.] I. New Moon (Duluth, Minn.)
GV709.N49   1999
796'.082—dc21   99-28712

10 9 8 7 6 5 4 3 2 1
First Edition

New Moon is a registered trademark of New Moon Publishing, Inc.

CONTENTS

The folks who made this book want to thank all the people who gave such enthusiastic help and who believe so strongly in Listening to Girls!

The Girls Editorial Board of *New Moon: The Magazine for Girls and Their Dreams,* the girls who read and create *New Moon* magazine, the New Moon Publishing team, and our parents.

Jennifer Cecil, Sheila Eldred, Seth Godin Productions, Bridget Grosser, Mavis Gruver, Debra Kass Orenstein, Joe Kelly, Nia Kelly, Erin Lyons, Jason Mandell, Deb Mylin, Sarah Silbert, Barbara Stretchberry, and Ann Weinerman.

Our colleagues at Lark Productions: Robin Dellabough, Lisa DiMona, and Karen Watts.

And our friends at Crown Publishing: Simon Boughton, Andrea Cascardi, Nancy Hinkel, and Isabel Warren-Lynch.

NOTE FROM *NEW MOON'S* FOUNDER

New Moon is a magazine that gives girls the power to believe in ourselves, to help us stand up for what we think is right, and, most of all, to let us just be girls. *New Moon* sends a message that makes a girl feel, "However I am, I'm okay." *New Moon* describes girls who take action when things are unfair, instead of keeping quiet. And *New Moon* is a fun, safe place where girls know that they are not alone.

New Moon: The Magazine for Girls and Their Dreams is an international, advertising-free bimonthly that is edited BY girls between ages 8 and 14. The recipient of dozens of awards, *New Moon* was twice named winner of the Parents' Choice Foundation Gold Award—the only child-edited magazine ever to win that honor. Begun in 1993, *New Moon* is a girl-driven alternative to magazines and other media that focus on how girls look. *New Moon's* slant is that makeup, boys, and fashion are important to girls, but they represent maybe three degrees of a girl's life. *New Moon* focuses on the other 357 degrees of a thinking girl's life. Instead of telling girls who they *should* be, *New Moon* tells the world who girls really *are*.

This series of New Moon Books continues that mission. Our books talk about real issues and real girls. They don't say, "This is how you have to be." Instead, they share girls' experiences, feelings, and ideas. Just like *New Moon* magazine, New Moon Books are created BY girls. We chose nine *New Moon* readers from all over the country, including Alaska and Hawaii, Minnesota and New York, to work on the books. They range in age from 10 to 14 and represent homeschool, public school, and private school. White, Black, Filipino, and Asian, these girls have done a marvelous job, as we knew they would.

In this book, they take a girl's-eye view of the dynamic world of sports. Working with Robin Dellabough of Lark Productions and Joe Kelly of New Moon Publishing, they've researched subjects from competition to body image, from attitude to how to improve. Jammed with profiles of real-life female athletes, the book also offers answers to a girl's real-life questions and concerns about sports, from both superstars and everyday people. Whether you throw, run, jump, glide, bat, hit, or roll, we think you'll find something to interest you in these pages. Our hope is that you'll want to stop reading and start moving.

We think you'll love this book because it's about how real girls play sports. So, get ready to find out more about sports by Listening to Girls, which is our favorite thing to do!

Molly McKinnon
Editor, *New Moon: The Magazine for Girls and Their Dreams*

Nancy Gruver
Founder & Publisher, New Moon Publishing

# Note from the New Moon Books Girls Editorial Board

We are very proud to be the Girls Editorial Board for these books. We hope that they will help other girls feel good about themselves and their abilities. Like you, we are strong, spirited girls. We got together at a hotel in New York to start creating the books. We had an awesome weekend, where we worked hard and played hard. We came up with ideas for most of the material in the books and had a say in everything that went into them. We chose topics that we wanted to write about, too. After that, we worked on the books and with each other over the Internet. And when each book was almost finished, we edited it and said what should change. All in all, it was a pretty amazing experience!

We appreciate New Moon's approach and feel lucky to be reaching more girls through this series of books. Sure, some of us may like boys and putting on makeup, but we also enjoy playing sports, spending time with our friends, learning about international happenings, reading, writing, and all of the other exciting things the world has to offer. That's why we researched and wrote about friendship, earning money, reading, writing, and sports — things that are important to girls in their lives. We found, in the United States and around the world, girls with competence and self-respect. We hope that you will find, in their experiences, the inspiration that every girl needs. Girls are so much more than clothes and diets; we are individuals with views and ideas, energy and talent. New Moon is our voice. Add yours and let us be heard!

Flynn Berry, age 11, New York

Lauren Calhoun, age 13, Hawaii

Ashley Cofell, age 10, Minnesota

Morgan Fykes, age 12, Washington, D.C.

Katie Hedberg, age 11, Minnesota

Elizabeth Larsson, age 12, New Jersey

Priscilla Mendoza, age 11, California

Julia Peters-Axtell, age 14, Minnesota

Caitlin Stern, age 13, Alaska

CHAPTER ONE

A Sporting Chance

Drive by most any playing field in a suburb, town, or city on a Saturday morning in spring, summer, or fall, and what do you see? Girls, boys, little kids, big kids, grownups, kicking, batting, or pitching some kind of ball around, while their families cheer or yell from the sidelines. Why aren't they home sleeping late or watching Saturday morning cartoons, or running errands downtown? Because these amateur athletes are having a blast out there, competing against each other or against themselves.

Not so long ago — just a few years ago, really — most of these hometown athletes, as well as the big-time college and pro athletes on television, were boys or men. Not anymore. If you take another look at those local Saturday morning players or the runners or the bicyclists zooming by, there's a pretty even chance you'll find girls wearing those uniforms or the latest high-tech sports gear. Nowadays girls and sports go together just the way guys and sports went together a few decades back. Girls are signing up for sports big time, and big-time sports like basketball, tennis, and golf are signing up girls and women in growing numbers.

What are so many girls discovering about sports nowadays that boys discovered a long time ago? Writer-athlete Mariah Burton Nelson, a former Stanford University and professional basketball player turned sportswriter, has a lot to say about the thrill and challenges of being a female athlete. When girl meets sport, Mariah believes, female athletes get to *really speak out, live out loud, be outstanding, challenge each other, be physically fit, be healthy.* These are some of the best reasons for girls to get out there — on that bike, into the pool, or onto the playing fields.

Author of three books on women and sports, Mariah says: "It takes courage to be competitive, to be outstanding, to deal with opponents. It takes courage to live out loud." Coaches have to work hard to get girls to really speak out, explains Mariah. "On a basketball court you learn to use your voice. You say, 'Help,' or 'I'm in the middle,' or 'I'll get her.' It carries over into the classroom. Your voice matters.

"When you challenge somebody to compete with you, you're getting to know them," Mariah says. "An opponent is not an enemy. We challenge each other to do our best. Competition can be a form of love. If I'm a good player, I'm offering my opponent a gift, a way for her to improve, to be inspired to do better.

"You don't play in order to win. You lose and you live and you move on. Losing is a part of what happens on the way to success. Professional basketball players miss about fifty percent of the time.

3

"I encourage everybody to be physically fit, even if they don't play a sport. We need to take care of these bodies we live in, not to be beautiful but to be healthy. If a woman swims or does aerobics or yoga, she should call herself an athlete. It's a good, strong word. There's nothing male or female about it. The more you think like an athlete, the more you'll act like an athlete."

Mariah Burton Nelson, who played big-league basketball in the seventies and eighties, is just one of the millions of female athletes who got a big boost in sports when the government passed the Title IX law. Thanks to Title IX, girls began to get the same opportunities boys had to participate in school sports.

Did You Know?

Congress passed a federal law called Title IX of the Education Amendments Act in 1972. Title IX says any junior high, high school, or college that receives money from the government cannot discriminate on the basis of gender in the provision of any educational activity—and that includes athletics. Title IX requires that girls and boys have equal benefits and opportunities, including the following:

* the same quality of equipment, uniforms, and other supplies;
* equal practice fields and facilities;
* equal size and quality of locker rooms and training rooms;
* equal number of coaches;
* the same number of awards and awards banquets;
* cheerleaders and bands or pep rallies for girls' games;
* and the same quality of transportation to away games.

If you think your school is not treating girls and boys equally, the Feminist Majority Foundation suggests the following resources:

* Your school may have designated someone on staff to handle Title IX and gender equity complaints. Ask around for that person, and talk to her or him.
* If you cannot find someone at your school to talk to, call your state's department of education and ask for the person in charge of gender equity and Title IX issues.
* If you cannot find someone in your state's department of education to talk to, call one of the regional offices of the U.S. Department of Education's Office

for Civil Rights. (See the New Moon Web site, www.newmoon.org, for phone numbers.)

If you are still having trouble finding someone to talk to, call the U.S. Department of Education's national Office for Civil Rights Complaint Investigation, 330 C St. SW, Washington, DC 20202, (202) 205-5413.

While Title IX opened the door for female athletes, some myths about girls and sports didn't completely disappear. Let's clear up some of those myths with science facts about females and sports.

Sports Myths: Truth or Dare

MYTH: Boys are better at sports than girls.

SCIENCE: Before girls and boys reach puberty, there aren't any physical differences that affect athletic ability. Girls can throw a baseball just as hard or jump just as high as boys — if they get equal training and practice.

There are sports that girls and women are better at, there are sports that boys and men are better at, and there are sports where gender simply doesn't matter. Although women have not competed for nearly as many years as men, some women are already equal to or surpass men in several sports. Ultra-marathoner Ann Trason won the Western States 100-mile race several times. And Julie Krone became the first female jockey to win a Triple Crown race when she cruised to a victory on Colonial Affair at the Belmont Stakes in 1993.

MYTH: Men have stronger muscles than women.

SCIENCE: The quality of muscle in men and women is identical. The difference comes in the amount and length of muscle. (Women have lower percentages of muscle and higher percentages of body fat, which they need in order to have children.) While men have a higher percentage of muscle, most girls and women are more flexible.

MYTH: Sweating means you're working harder and cooling off better.

SCIENCE: In endurance events, men start sweating earlier than women. When people first discovered this, they assumed that it was better to sweat earlier. Later studies showed that although men sweat earlier (which allows them to cool off quickly), they are also more likely to sweat too

7

much (when sweat drips from your skin, it stops cooling you off). Sweating less gives women an advantage over men in hot, wet conditions. So, along with their higher percentage of body fat, this gives women an edge in super-endurance sports, like marathon swimming and ultra-marathon running, where the top women often compete equally alongside the top men.

Did You Know?

There are over 10,000 athletic scholarships available to women in U.S. colleges each year.

Even in countries without the Title IX law to level the sports playing fields, girls are determined to get strong and compete. Here's how a young Palestinian woman's determination to compete in a male sport got her to the championship level.

POINT OF VIEW: *Cycling for Peace*

I am Palestinian, and I live in Ramallah, in the West Bank. One summer as I was passing my boyfriend's house, I remembered the first time we met. He had fallen off his bike, and I helped him get up. All of a sudden, I thought about getting a bike of my own.

The general idea in Ramallah is: "Bikes are not for girls." In the beginning, I deliberately made myself look like a boy as I cycled. Then I discovered that I was trying to hide the only special thing about myself. I was trying to make people accept me rather than simply accepting myself.

Throughout the year, I trained myself for Ramallah's cycling race. I won this race and was surprised to be chosen as my country's coordinator of the Great Millennium Peace Ride, a two-year cycling trip around the world. The Great Millennium Peace Ride will include cyclists from all over the world.

—Shuruq, age 15, Israel

❝What do you do if someone is always saying you can't play a sport because you are a girl?❞

1. Short & sweet: Don't listen to them.

2. More complete: Show them what you can do. If you prove to them that you can meet the requirements of the sport, they will probably stop. If they don't, just tune them out. Their prejudice will hurt them the most in the end. ◇

Choosing Your Sport

There are dozens of sports for girls to choose from. How do you decide which sport is the right one for you? Here are some questions to consider:

* What sports do your school, town, and local sports clubs offer?

* Do you need lessons for the sports you think you like? If you do, is there enough money for lessons? Can you get a ride to and from the lessons?

★ What equipment or clothes do you need to get
  started?

★ What sports can you do on your own without
  lessons, fancy equipment, or transportation?

To help you think about what kinds of sports might ap-
peal to you, here's an informal checklist to fill out.

Good Sports: A Checklist

I'd Rather Do My Sport: Sports You Might Like

___outdoors   baseball, outdoor basketball,
                            biking, canoeing, diving,
                            hiking, kayaking, field hockey,
                            football, golf, handball, horse-
                            back riding, outdoor ice
                            hockey, ice skating, jumping
                            rope, rollerblading, running,
                            skiing, snowboarding, soccer,
                            softball, speed skating, surfing,
                            swimming, tennis, walking,
                            water-skiing   **11**

A Sporting Chance

___ indoors

indoor basketball, dancing, diving, fencing, gymnastics, indoor ice hockey, indoor ice skating, martial arts, racquetball, squash, swimming, volleyball, yoga

___ in water

canoeing, diving, fishing, kayaking, rafting, rowing, snorkeling, swimming

___ on a sidewalk

biking, rollerblading, running, skateboarding, street hockey, walking

I'll only play if it's:

___ just me

diving, golf, gymnastics, hiking, ice skating, jumping rope, kayaking, martial arts, rollerblading, running, skateboarding, skiing, snow-boarding, surfing, swimming, walking, water-skiing, yoga

___ me and you   canoeing, dancing, fencing, handball, racquetball, rafting, squash, singles tennis

___ me and the gang   baseball, basketball, field hockey, football, ice hockey, lacrosse, soccer, softball, doubles tennis, volleyball

___ me and an animal   dogsledding, horseback riding

If you want to find out more about some of these sports, you'll find in Chapter Six a list of books, organizations, and Web pages where you can get all the information you need to find out about almost every sport — even some you may not have heard of. We've also scattered **Hot Tips for Hot Sports** throughout Chapters Two and Three. Check them out.

Did You Know?

In the early 1900s, undergarments worn under "sports clothes" were more dangerous than the sports themselves. Corsets (a body wrap from the hips to the chest with whalebone ribbing running vertically up the body) were pulled so tight around the waist that they made women faint regularly, and even dislodged organs! Women wore them so that they could have fashionably thin waists. The corset was used in swimming, bicycling, tennis, and exercising. Can you imagine running, swimming, bicycling, or playing tennis without being able to breathe? The corset was abandoned as more and more women got into sports.

In the 1920s, Annette Kellerman (a champion swimmer) and Suzanne Lenglen (a tennis star) each created more comfortable, practical clothes for their sports: body-hugging suits for swimming and shorter skirts for tennis. They wore their new outfits in public and were criticized, scorned, and even arrested for their daring. Only a few years later, though, their outfits were adopted by other women athletes.

CHAPTER TWO

Go Solo (or Almost)!

Are you someone who enjoys individual activities more than group activities — singing alone in the shower rather than in the choir? Or writing an article at home for the school paper rather than working on the editorial staff? Lots of sports — diving, golf, hiking, running, rollerblading, figure skating, skateboarding, skiing, and swimming, for example — offer plenty of challenge to girls who enjoy setting personal goals more than team goals — *my* mountain, *my* best time, *my* reverse dive.

No matter what solo sport attracts you, there are lots of ways to take any of these sports to another level. A hiker can become a mountain climber. A runner can train for a marathon. A kayaker paddling around the local pond can try out whitewater kayaking.

If you have a feeling the best competitor you'll ever face is *you,* then study this chart of solo sports. See where they can take you. And if you want some company once in a while, many of these sports offer that, too. Skateboard alone on your street, then join other skateboarders at the park. Bike to town — or to a town twenty miles away during a road race. Go solo just a little ways, or go as far as you want with your sport. It's your call.

The Basic Sport	Take It to the Next Level
Bicycling	Bike racing; mountain biking
Canoeing	Portaging (carrying your canoe through the woods on long trips)
Cross-country skiing	Cross-country ski racing
Dancing	Ballet company
Diving	Competitive diving
Figure skating	Competitive figure skating; ice dancing
Golf	Competitive golf
Gymnastics	Competitive gymnastics
Hiking	Climbing more difficult terrain; mountain climbing
Ice skating	Speed skating
Jumping rope	Competitive jump roping
Kayaking	Whitewater kayaking
Martial arts	Earning belts at higher levels of difficulty; tournaments
Rollerblading	Choreographed rollerblading; rollerblade competitions
Running	Road racing; long-distance or marathon running

Skateboarding	Skateboarding in special skate-board parks; skateboarding demonstrations
Surfing	Competitive surfing
Swimming	Swimming races; endurance swimming
Wheelchair racing	Paralympic Games

Strong Bodies, Good Hearts

Meet two individual-sport athletes, a runner and a mountain climber, who not only got their heart rates up training for their sports but also used their good hearts to raise money for worthy causes. If you would like to help the world and train in solo sports like running, swimming, or walking, check out the newspaper for walkathons, marathons, or swimathons where you can get your body in shape and the world in shape at the same time.

POINT OF VIEW: *Racing*

I enjoy running because after a run, I feel exhilarated, although tired. Did you know that exercise releases more endorphins, your "feel good" chemicals? I often run 5Ks with my parents. (A 5K is a race that is 5 kilometers, or 3.5 miles, long.) Last September, I ran Race for the Cure, a 5K in New York City's Central Park that raises money for the Susan G. Komen Foundation, which helps breast cancer patients. Oftentimes, women who run it are in remission from breast cancer. Also, you can run in someone's name and dedicate the race to her. It was very fun and festive, full of resilient women. Race for the Cure also puts a spin on the usual race: only women run, and men cheer them on from the sidelines. I've also run races around the local colleges, etc. The New York Road Runners Club is one way I find races. I'm sure your area has something like it.

—Flynn, age 11, New York

Hot Running Tips

✳ Concentrate! While running, pay attention to your form. Stay relaxed with your hands loose, your elbows close to your sides, and your weight equally distributed on both sides of your body.

✳ Breathe! Inhale deeply through your nose into your stomach, not only as far as your chest.

✳ Glide! Don't bounce off the balls of your feet, which will make you move up and down too much. Instead, think of gliding forward.

✳ Snack! A light snack, such as a plain bagel or a banana, is okay before a hard run, but don't eat a big meal for three or more hours beforehand.

✳ Drink! Stay hydrated by drinking plenty of water before, during, and after a hard run.

POINT OF VIEW: *Mountain Climbing*

Alaska's Mt. McKinley, or Denali, is the highest mountain in North America. On average, only about half of the people who try to climb it reach the summit (top). And the average age of Denali's climbers is thirty-two.

On June 23 at 11:35 p.m., I stood on top of Denali. I was twelve and a half years old—the youngest person ever to climb Denali. I had dreamed of climbing this 20,320-foot mountain since I was nine. My mom didn't take me seriously until I was about eleven. From then on, my mom and I worked to get a climbing group together. After finding six others who wanted to climb Denali, including a guide, we started getting our gear together, training, and talking.

My training included: gymnastics, hiking, skiing, and snowboarding (a lot of what I was already doing). When my mom and I hiked, we carried packs and hauled sleds. We increased our loads each time we hiked. We climbed Mt. Goode (11,000 feet) to get more glacier-climbing experience.

My big climb began when I arrived at Denali's base camp on June 2. Even though I was in what looked like a winter wonderland, the weather was sweltering hot. In order to take all of the

gear, fuel, and food that we needed, we towed our supplies be-
hind us in sleds. (I hauled anywhere from forty to sixty pounds!)

After reaching camp, we then hauled our extra loads ahead
to our next day's camp, buried them in what's called a "cache,"
and then returned down the mountain to set up our present
camp and spend the night. The next day, if the weather was
good, we packed up our camp and climbed back to where we
had "cached" our supplies. So, in reality, we climbed the mountain twice!

Most days, we climbed for five to six hours and then spent
four hours setting up camp. We did that routine over and over
until we reached our camp at 17,000 feet—our last camp. We
planned to go to the top the next day, but we got snowed in at
"17" for a week.

We finally went when the weather was right. It was a really
warm morning. But when we climbed around the corner, it got
much colder, and the wind picked up incredibly fast. We hiked
for a few hours in the clouds—I couldn't even see my feet.
When we got to 19,000 feet, it was about twenty degrees
below zero! There, we took a break and put on some more
clothes.

Walking along the summit ridge felt like climbing a staircase to heaven. I couldn't see what I was stepping on, but when I looked up, my mind was clear of all thoughts. We hiked the last hundred feet to the summit. It felt like we were on top of the clouds. I was the first one to touch the summit, something I will never forget.

I didn't climb just for myself. I wanted my climb to benefit others somehow. I decided to raise money for the Anchorage Center for Families. Supporters pledged money for every check-point I reached while climbing. In the end, I collected $4,500.

I want to inspire girls to do what they dream. But you have to think things through. Prepare for your dreams.

—Merrick, age 14, Alaska

Solo Sports – the Four-Legged Kind

If you're a dog owner, you've probably heard *Take the dog out!* more than once. Well, Jessica Royer takes *sixteen* dogs out and travels hundreds of miles with them through the frigid Minnesota landscape. Jessica is a sled-dog racer, or *musher,* in a sport that requires tremendous endurance, hard work, planning skills, and a sense of authority to "lead the pack."

HIGH PROFILE: JESSICA ROYER

Preparing herself and her dogs is the most important part of sled-dog racing, Jessica says. Training the dogs involves feeding them balanced meals, keeping them healthy, and taking them out on runs. "I take them out on thirty- and forty-mile runs to get their endurance up," she says.

Just before a race, Jessica gets all her gear and sleds ready. Of course, the dogs come first — they have to be all there and in working order, too! Before hooking the dogs up to the line, Jessica looks everything over one last time and gets checked by race officials. It is the last step before she and her dogs explode onto the course at the starting signal.

On the trail, she uses simple commands: "When I want them to go, I say, 'Let's go.' 'Gee' is right, and 'Haw' is left. When we come to a road crossing or I see other dogs or wildlife around, I tell them, 'Straight ahead!' The dogs continue on their path, and they won't bother the wildlife."

While she races, Jessica concentrates on how the dogs are doing and thinks about what's ahead. She must be prepared for anything, whether it's thin ice or moose on the trail. She also must anticipate upcoming checkpoints: she thinks about what she wants to do there so that she'll be back on the trail as soon as possible.

Jessica is deciding if she wants to train her dogs for the thousand-mile Iditarod, in Alaska. "That would be a neat race to enter," she says.

—Kaitlin, age 13, and Ana, age 14, Minnesota

Everybody into the Water

Some girls are all wet. If you're a "water baby" and can't just sit on the pool deck or on the ocean shore without jumping in, meet two young women who spend as much time as they can training solo on water or plunging through it.

HIGH PROFILE: MARGO OBERG

Margo Oberg, a former world champion surfer, taught me how to surf at the break near Poipu, on Kauai. When I fell off a wave, I'd paddle back out, and there was Margo reassuring me.

Margo won her first contest when she was eleven. "I lived right on the beach in La Jolla, California. I was in a club called Junior Oceanographers, and we went out on the pier and caught fish, so all I wanted to do was surf." By age fifteen, Margo was the best amateur surfer on the West Coast. Then she got invited to the World Title in Puerto Rico and won. She was the best amateur in the world. In 1975, she turned pro.

Because waves are always changing, always different, a surfer has to adjust all of the time. Margo believes that after you get the basics down, you develop your own style. "It's sort of like dancing or the martial arts. You develop your own stance. The wave is always the factor."

—Lauren, age 13, Hawaii

Of course, there's more than one way to get wet — or not — sports-wise. You can work out *on* the water. That's what river rafting guide Kate Rineer has done for the last twenty years.

HIGH PROFILE: KATE RINEER

Kate Rineer first started river rafting as a hobby with friends in Utah, learning by trial and error. There weren't any rafting schools when she started, so the only way to learn was to do it.

As a rafting guide for Mountain Travel Sobek, Kate gets to experience beautiful, remote areas, only accessible by water. River rafting is also physically demanding, requiring high energy and the ability to endure rain, wind, and cold for possibly all of the trip.

An exciting experience in rafting is doing a first descent—being the first to raft in a certain area. There is no information from previous trips to go by, so the guides must do an aerial survey and study the geology to see if a trip is possible.

Being tough and competitive is a job requirement, and not something that comes naturally to Kate. Kate says that she has had an easier time being accepted by male rafters than some women have. Rafting was so new in Alaska when she started out that no rules had been set; it was all new ground.

Kate has rafted on every continent except Australia, and has learned about the geology, flora, fauna, history, religions, and languages of many of them. For girls interested in rafting, Kate recommends going on a river trip with a guide. Being guided down a river is a safe way to find out if you really want to be a rafter.

—Caitlin, age 13, Alaska

Another Kind of Challenge

Some solo sports, like wheelchair racing, are open only to athletes with physical challenges. Though these athletes may train alone, they don't compete alone. LeAnn Shannon, a thirteen-year-old wheelchair racer from Orange Park, Florida, was the youngest competitor at the 1996 Olympics and 1996 Paralympics, in Atlanta, Georgia, where she won three gold medals and broke two world records. The Paralympics began in 1960; they give athletes who are physically challenged a chance for a gold medal. Another outstanding Paralympics participant is Maggie Behle, who hasn't let the fact she was born with one leg stop her from excelling as a skier.

HIGH PROFILE: MAGGIE BEHLE

Imagine racing down a steep snow-covered mountain at top speed, trying to zip your skis in and out of gates with no room for error. Total concentration or total wipeout. Now imagine doing it with one leg! Maggie Behle's mother was a ski racer, and Maggie never thought about not becoming one herself. She never thought of herself as being disabled. She is, in fact, very ABLE.

Maggie and her American teammates competed at the Winter Olympics in Nagano, Japan, when Maggie was seventeen years old. Maggie competes in the LW-2 class—she's a three-tracker. A three-tracker skis on one leg with two outriggers (ski poles with little skis attached to them). According to Maggie, three-trackers have the advantage in slalom because they can turn a lot faster than people with two legs.

Maggie brought two bronze medals home from Nagano, in the slalom and downhill races. Maggie says, "You turn a lot more in slalom and you have to be really aggressive. You have to concentrate a lot because it is really easy to miss a gate, and if you miss a gate, you're disqualified from the race." But Maggie likes downhill best. "It's not my best because I'm so short, but I love going really fast."

Maggie started skiing when she was four. She says she was a little scared on the first day, but she liked the challenge of bigger and bigger hills. "I kind of got better and better, and the better I got at skiing, the more I wanted to do more challenging things." Eventually Maggie was winning all kinds of races. When she started beating Olympic team members at the age of thirteen, she was chosen to be a part of the Olympic team.

To all girls who are interested in ski racing, Maggie gives the following advice: "Make sure you're having fun and not doing it because you're competitive. Do it because you really love it."

—Lauren, age 13, Hawaii

Ask a Girl

"How can I prove to others that I play in a wheelchair just as well as, if not better than, they play? Whenever I try to play, everyone just laughs. Help."

You must be playing with the wrong people! Some of the BEST athletes have physical challenges. Maybe you could practice one-on-one with someone and then have that person introduce you to the others. Once you've shown one person, you may not need to convince anyone else! ◈

Personal Best

If you like personal challenges and the convenience of training on your own, solo sports are great. But watch out! If you get good enough, you won't be solo for long. You could be standing on a podium while the crowd cheers and an official places a gold medal — or five — around your neck. That's what happened to Olympic speed skater Bonnie Blair, who won five gold medals in three Olympic games—more than any other female U.S. Olympic athlete.

HIGH PROFILE: BONNIE BLAIR

New Moon: At what age did you become serious about speed skating?

Bonnie Blair: I was racing at the age of four, but around age sixteen or seventeen, I made a decision to become more dedicated to the sport.

NM: How do you motivate yourself before a race?

BB: I approach every race in the same way, like it's the Olympics. I go through the same preparation, whether it's mental or physical, so when I get to the big competitions, I'm prepared.

NM: How does it feel to win a gold medal?

BB: I think each win had its different meaning. My first gold medal definitely was the most powerful and emotional because, I think, doing something for the very first time captures feelings that aren't repeated. There were so many different emotions going through me at once. In Lillehammer, it was more of a sad feeling because I knew it was the last time that I'd be able to do that. I knew it was the end.

Go Solo (or Almost)!

NM: What do you think your role is in helping girls realize their potential?

BB: I think girls need to find the one thing that they enjoy. When you have a passion for something, working hard for a goal is easier. Sports made me try and get better grades in school, because if I wanted to go to the different events at school, my parents made me get good grades. I started competing within myself for grades. I found I became a better person. It started out in sports and carried on into the rest of the areas of my life.

—Ana, age 14, Minnesota

Hot Ice-Skating Tips

* Dance! Dancing helps you coordinate movement with music.

* Run! Long-distance running builds endurance and develops the kind of balance you need for skating.

* Sign up! If you're serious about ice skating, inquire about lessons at a local rink or skating school.

Passion for the sport plus the inner competition Bonnie Blair talks about — "competing within myself" — drive champions in other solo sports as well. See if you've got what it takes!

How to Be a Solo Player

No matter what sport we choose, girls like us find ways to make athletics more fun, help us improve, and stay motivated.

✳ Set a mini-goal for yourself every time you train — a quarter lap more, a pound more on the weight bar, one less golf stroke on a hole.

✳ Keep a notebook or mark a calendar to chart your progress.

✳ Find a cheerleader to applaud your progress — a sibling, a parent, a friend.

✳ Share your skills. Check out whether there are any groups you can join once in a while — the local road-racing bike club, a skateboarding group that meets at the local park, an outdoor hiking group.

CHAPTER THREE

Go, Team!

The team. My team. Our team. What a special sound those words have. A group of girls, arm in arm, huddled around their coach before a big game. Opposing teams going down two lines after the game, slapping each other's palms, and saying: "Good game. Good game. Good game." That hugging circle of teammates after a tough defeat. These become powerful memories for us athletes. We become part of something bigger than ourselves and our sport. Being on a team combines intense shared experiences, cooperation, relationships, feelings, and skills.

Girls and Competition

A team is a kind of family. Just as in a family, there are hugs and squabbles, unity and competition. Sometimes girls are reluctant to join a team because of the emphasis on winning. Pressure is on for girls to show that they can be tough and aggressive enough to compete in sports. Can girls take the good side of competition without the bad?

Donna A. Lopiano, Ph.D., Executive Director of the Women's Sports Foundation, says: "Sport gives you experience so you learn to win graciously and accept defeat without blowing the experience out of proportion. You learn to separate the outcome of a game or your performance in one game from your worth as a person."

While there is nothing like the joy of a great win, there is a lot of good in losing, too, believe it or not. Instead of beating up on ourselves, we can help each other learn from defeat if someone — the coach, the captain, or any team member — says: "Hey, we lost, but did you see that cool defense move they did? Let's try that in the next game." You win whenever you learn something new about the game or about yourself.

Winning and Losing— It Is How the Game Is Played

If you're thinking about whether team sports are for you, read on. Here are a few girls who might convince you that team competition can bring out the best in you.

"To be on the losing team in a championship game feels sad," says Ashley. "I usually don't make a big deal about it. I just say to myself, 'Better luck next year,' and go home happy. I know a girl who has never been to the championship level, so I'm just happy to have been in the championship game. I still like to play even after I've lost,

Hot Soccer Tips

* Lock your ankle when passing.

* Always wear shin guards.

* If you're a goalie, use your hands *and* your body.

* Warm up before the game/practice.

* Always bring H_2O to games/practices.

* During a throw-in, stand between the receiver and the goal.

* Come at a right angle to the person you're passing to.

* Be aggressive.

—Priscilla, age 11, California

because I love the sport almost as much as I love winning."

"I was always on a losing team," Julia recalls. "It didn't feel good, because I knew that I tried my hardest and some other girls did, too. All the work and practice does pay off sooner or later. I have to not forget that. I have to remember the most important thing is that we played well and had fun. I play soccer after all those years of losing because I just like the thought of playing my sport. It would be nice to win more games, but I think, 'Am I having fun playing this sport?' And I am."

Remember, even if your team loses, you can still win big if you and your teammates keep learning from your mistakes.

What if you want to do a sport but you're not sure whether you want to train with a team all the time? Find out by reading about one athlete — a weight lifter — who competes against herself when she trains but shows off her stuff as part of a team, too!

HIGH PROFILE: LISA TAYLOR-PARISI

Thirteen-year-old Lisa Taylor-Parisi practices her "clean and jerk" every week. No, she's not helping out with house-cleaning. Lisa is on a weightlifting team in Essex, Vermont. The "clean and jerk" is a style of lifting weights.

Less than a year after starting to lift weights, Lisa tied the Teenage New England record in the clean and jerk by lifting eighty-eight pounds. Lisa weighs just ninety-two pounds herself! She credits her ten years of ballet with helping her weightlifting technique.

How did Lisa get interested in such a heavy hobby? Her coach, Chris Polakowski, known as Mr. Pol, is also her gym teacher. One day he was watching Lisa work the rings during gymnastics. "I was impressed with her natural strength. I suggested that she try weightlifting, and I'm happy to say she took me up on it," says Mr. Pol. "Lisa's explosive. That's probably the number one requirement for this kind of lifting—speed. Lisa's got it."

Since Lisa began lifting, she has accomplished a lot. She has already won the bronze medal in her weight class at the Junior National Weightlifting Championship in Albuquerque, New Mexico. Not too shabby for someone new to her sport!

Good competition was exactly what another stand-out athlete got when she joined the formerly all-male Harlem Globetrotters. The legendary professional basketball team got even better after Jolette "Jazzy" Law arrived on the court.

HIGH PROFILE: JOLETTE LAW

New Moon: How did you get started with the Harlem Globetrotters?

Jolette Law: After graduating from college, in 1990, I tried out to represent the U.S. at the Goodwill Games. Scouts from the Harlem Globetrotters were there. As a kid, I grew up loving the Globetrotters, watching them on television, seeing them on *Scooby-Doo*. Whenever they would come to town, my mother and father would take me. Well, the scouts invited me to their camp, and the rest is history.

NM: How does it feel being the only woman on the team?

JL: It gives me a heartwarming feeling to go out each and every night and let these guys know that women can do things, too.

NM: Do you feel like you had to be better than the guys to be able to make it? More skilled?

41

JL: I had to develop skills that were patented Jolette. They saw I was a female and said, "Oh, she can't shoot." I'm short for a basketball player [5'4"], so that was a disadvantage. So I had to get my ball-handling skills together. When I go up to the hole, I have this little scoop shot that all the guys swing at and miss.

NM: Do you have any advice for girls who would like to play sports?

JL: You can try anything. If you feel comfortable within yourself, just believe that you will achieve. Most everywhere I go, the women come to me after the game. Now even most of the boys say, "Wow, you're cool, you're awesome. Man, Jazz, you're my favorite player."

—Erin, age 13, and Amanda, age 11, Minnesota

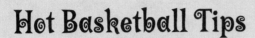

Hot Basketball Tips

* Shoot! Practice shooting from different points on the court. Start near the basket and gradually move farther away as you become more confident.

* Dribble! Practice dribbling, using each hand. That way, you'll be able to move in all directions with the ball, and defenders won't know which way to stop you from going.

* Drill! A good drill is to run between the free-throw line and the baseline (the boundary under the basket at the end of the court). Touch each line with your hand every time you get to it. Then try doing the same between the half-court line and the baseline, and then from one baseline to the other. This will help improve your quickness, your stamina, and your leg muscles.

43

Ask a Girl

"I'm not very good at sports, and I don't enjoy playing them. I have to be on a sports team for school, though. How can I try to enjoy playing sports and make the most out of my experience?"

1. *Believe in yourself. Have confidence. Say to yourself, "I can do this."*
2. *Participate—force yourself to get in the game.*
3. *Practice, practice, practice.*
4. *Most important, have fun!* ◇

Having Attitude

Attitude is important in any sport, but especially in team sports. Attitude, good or bad, is contagious. A positive attitude spreads through the team to help them work together. A bad attitude brings everyone down. It affects how you play and how the teammates perform as a group. When your attitude is good and you support your team, you get

44 pumped up and play better.

These few things will help you improve as one person and as a team. Remember, there is no *I* in *TEAM*.

How to Be a Team Player

* Support your teammates even when they mess up. Find something positive to say, even after a bad play: "Hey, we wouldn't have gotten as far as we did without all the great plays you made in the first quarter. Everybody's off sometimes."

* Try your hardest. If you lose the game, you will still know that you did your very best. Then there will be no "if only"!

* Pass the ball, the puck, the birdie!

* Stay open to your coach's advice.

* Share the spotlight even if you are the highest scorer.

* Share tips, not blame. Bad feelings infect future games. Good tips boost team spirit.

* Cheer before, during, and after the game. Cheering gets you pumped up and helps you finish the game on a "high."

✷ Never give up. Miracles happen every day! If you don't give up, you'll still have a chance (even though it's a thin one) at anything! You'll also feel better about the game overall. *Try it;* you'll know what we mean!

Did You Know?

80% of women identified in a survey as key leaders in successful corporations participated in sports during their childhood and identified themselves as having been "tomboys."

CHAPTER FOUR

Your Body:
An Owner's Manual

Do you know what to do if you get injured during a sport? Or how to avoid getting hurt in the first place? Do you know which foods help you build strength and which ones give you quick energy? Read on! This chapter is jammed with information that will help you stay healthy and fit so you can keep playing your favorite sports!

Stay in the Game

Did you know that each year about ten percent of physically active people have at least one sports-related injury? If you're a girl who does sports, chances are you won't be able to avoid ever being hurt. But you can prevent being sidelined too often by following these suggestions:

Warm Up, So You Don't Burn Out

A lot of people, including adults, skip stretching both before and after exercise because they find it boring. Remember, though, it's much more boring to get hurt and not be able to play your sport! Your body is like any machine: its muscles and joints need to warm up before being used. Then they need to cool down after heavy use so you don't cramp up or get too sore the next day.

Use the Right Stuff

Wearing different shoes for tennis, for example, than you do for soccer is key to providing the kind of support your foot needs for that type of movement. If you aren't sure of the correct equipment for your sport, check with your coach or gym teacher or contact one of the organizations in the resource section on pages 85–86.

Play Right

If a movement or exercise feels unnatural or odd, chances are you're not doing it properly. For instance, when you run, it should feel comfortable each time your foot touches the ground. If you're running incorrectly—without good form—you may feel pain, which could lead to foot and ankle injuries. Again, ask your coach or teacher to make sure you're moving the best way for your sport.

Easy Does It

You don't have to work out at full speed every single day. Even top athletes switch hard training days with easier ones. If you don't give your body recovery time, you may

49

wind up with an injury. When you start to feel pain or feel dizzy or breathless, STOP.

Just (Don't) Do It

If you feel sick or hurt, don't play. Learn to listen to yourself and your own body more than you listen to anyone else, including your coach or even your parents. One twelve-year-old girl we know couldn't stand the thought of missing an important soccer game — even though she knew she was coming down with something. She forced herself to play. But then she got so sick, she missed the next *two* games. If she had taken care of herself in the first place, maybe her cold wouldn't have turned into bronchitis.

Get Enough Sleep and Take Time Off

The more active you are, the more sleep you'll need. Experiment with what the ideal amount is for you, and then try to stick to that every night. Your body will appreciate at least a day or two a week of complete rest, as well.

Pay Attention to the Weather

Is it humid, hot, cold, or pouring outside? Before you work out or go to a game, check out the conditions, then adapt. If it's sweltering, you'll know to wear your lightest clothes and bring extra water. If you hear thunder and see lightning, of course you'll know to stay inside!

Cross-Train

Instead of swimming every day, try running or riding a bike. The change will work a different set of muscles, and that will help keep you from getting injured because of overusing the same old muscles. Also, if you hurt one part of your body—say, your knees—cross-training gives you a backup activity while you let yourself heal.

Body Parts

Here are some ways to help keep the most vulnerable parts of your body from getting hurt in sports. To learn the correct stretches for each area, check one of the many books or Web sites listed on pages 82–84 or ask a teacher or coach.

Knees

Stretch your legs every day with knee-stretching and knee-strengthening exercises. Stretched and flexible leg muscles protect the knee much better than tight and inflexible muscles. Pay special attention to building balanced strength in the leg muscles (the quadriceps and hamstrings) that support and surround the knee. The stronger they are, the less stress on your knee joint. Many knee injuries come from trying to do too much, too fast, on legs that are not strong or flexible enough to take the stress.

Elbows

The best thing you can do to prevent tennis elbow is to not depend on tennis alone to work your elbow. Lack of strength in your forearm muscles, for example, can lead to tendinitis, so do exercises off-court to increase your forearm strength and flexibility. Good playing technique is important, too. If your arm begins to ache while playing, cut back on playing time until your tendons have a chance to recover. Make sure your racket fits (not too big, too small, or too heavy). A large-headed racket may give you a bigger "sweet spot" for better hitting, but if it's too heavy to position easily, what good does it do?

Hamstrings

One of the most common athletic injuries involves the hamstrings, which are at the back of your thighs. The best way to prevent hamstring muscle pulls is to stretch leg muscles thoroughly before exercising and to keep in shape. Before stretching, you may want to walk briskly or jog slowly for five to ten minutes to warm the muscles. If you hurt your hamstring, lie on your stomach and apply an ice pack to the back of your thigh. When the pain subsides, stretch and condition the muscles before exercise.

Ankles

If you're an athlete, you want to keep away from high heels, platform shoes, and floppy sandals, all of which leave you more prone to ankle sprains. Wear good, stable shoes that give your feet (and ankles) enough support and cushioning. Don't exercise in worn-out workout shoes.

Strength and flexibility are the best ways to prevent

Did You Know?

Strong hands make stronger golfers, basketball and volleyball players, etc. To increase the strength of your grip, squish some Silly Putty whenever you happen to think of it during your day: when you're on the phone, watching TV, stuck in the car, whatever. Just squeeze and release for two to four minutes, three to five times a day.

ankle sprains. Tight calf muscles pull on your Achilles tendon, which is connected to the heel bone, so keep your calf muscles stretched and flexible.

To strengthen your ankles (especially if you've already had an ankle injury), try heel walking: while wearing flat shoes, stand on your heels, keeping your toes as high off the ground as you can. Walk around for a few minutes. Then walk on your toes with your heels up in the air. Walk around on the insides of your feet. Then the outsides. If any of this hurts, don't do it!

If you *do* hurt your ankle, follow the R-I-C-E rule:

Rest

Ice

Compression

Elevation

Apply ice for five to ten minutes for the first 24 to 72 hours after the injury. Wrap your ankle firmly but not too tightly with an elastic bandage—that's compression. And keep your ankle higher than your hip.

Muscle Cramps

Sometimes called spasms, muscle cramps can come on so suddenly you don't know what's hit you. And they can happen to anyone, no matter what shape you're in, and anywhere, even in bed! If you've ever been running down a soccer field and felt a sharp blade in the middle of your leg, you know what a muscle cramp feels like. Muscles that are worked for too long or too hard can get a cramp. Not drinking enough liquids can cause muscle cramps, too. Sometimes a muscle will cramp right away and sometimes it will cramp later, at night.

What can you do? Gently massage the painful area. If the cramp is in your calf (the most common place to be hit), flex your foot upward. This contracts the muscle in front of your shin and relaxes your calf. Lying down and grabbing your toes and the ball of your foot and gently pulling them toward your knee may help, too. Sometimes ice, or in cold weather a hot towel, applied during stretching can help relieve a cramp, especially if an injury is involved.

To keep those nasty cramps at bay, try to massage the part of your body that tends to cramp, after sports and right before you go to bed. As always, stretch your calf muscles before and after you work out, too. Drink before, during, and after a workout: you need plenty of water, and more if you're participating in a long athletic event in the heat. Eat foods high in potassium—bananas, oranges, fresh vegetables.

You Are What You Eat

A well-balanced diet is important for everyone, from a high jumper to a couch potato. But an athlete uses up her vitamins, minerals, and calories faster because she burns more energy. So athletes can and should eat more of the healthy foods that everyone needs.

Whether you're an athlete already, or thinking about becoming one, here are a few places you can start looking to get information about healthy eating habits:

Eat Smart: A Guide to Good Health for Kids, by Dale Figtree and John McDougall (New Win Publishing, 1997)

Nutrition for Dummies (first edition), by Carol Ann Rinzler (IDG Worldwide, 1997)

The Nutrition-Fitness Link: How Diet Can Help Your Body and Mind (A Teen Nutrition Book), by Charles A. Salter (Millbrook Press, 1993)

The Right Moves: A Girl's Guide to Getting Fit and Feeling Good, by Tina Schwager and Michele Schuerger (Free Spirit Publishing, 1998)

www.healthfinder.org
This is a government-sponsored Web site chock-full of information on all kinds of topics, including a lot on nutrition.

Got Milk?

Milk doesn't just give you cute moustaches. The calcium in milk and in some other foods helps you build the bones you'll need for the rest of your life. The calcium you consume now helps your bones stay strong later—think of it as depositing coins in a piggy bank for your body. It's especially important for young women to get calcium, because women's bones are more likely to become brittle later in life.

Everyone loses calcium every day, and it needs to be replaced every day, too. Milk, cheese, and yogurt are the obvious places to get the daily calcium you need. However, if you're allergic to dairy products or you can't fit in dairy products three times a day, here are some other good sources of calcium.

Beans

Broccoli

Corn tortillas

Dried figs

Fortified orange juice (check the label)

Squash

How to Eat Before You Compete

If you've been eating right regularly, your body has fuel on hand for most of your sports activities. However, many sports nutritionists suggest that adding extra carbohydrates to a healthy diet helps give athletes an added boost the day before a big sports event.

If you want to pack in some extra fuel before a big workout or game, the kinds of foods you eat *the twelve or so hours before* a competition can help you "fuel up" for more endurance. As we said before, you are what you eat.

So eat a balanced diet most of the time. Then include some of the following foods *about twelve hours before* your big competition or workout.

potatoes

rice

pasta

whole-grain bread

The day before your game and right up to it, hold the fats, which slow down your metabolism. Lay off gassy foods, like broccoli, beans, and cabbage. Also avoid salads and fruits, which can cause diarrhea when your body is pushed to the limit. A little salt is okay, but not too much, since you don't want to get dehydrated.

Good-Timing Tips

★ Plan to have your biggest meal, with plenty of carbo-hydrates, the *night before* your event.

★ Try not to eat less than two hours before your heavy-duty exercise or event.

★ If you must have something to eat before a sports event, keep it light — crackers and fruit juices will take

59

the edge off your appetite without making you feel nauseated or heavy.

* Drink more than you think you need — at least several cups of water before and right after your event. For long-distance sports, like marathon running or swimming, drink plenty of water while you are moving.

* Those fruits you didn't eat right before your game? Enjoy them a few hours after your event to replace the potassium you lost if you sweated a lot. In other words, have a banana!

Did You Know?

It's best to drink at least two full glasses of water before you exercise, and at least that much during and after your activity. Your body is losing fluids even if you're not sweating. And if your urine is dark yellow, you're not drinking enough! If plain water is too bland, mix in some fruit juice.

Body Image

Open a magazine. Go to a movie. Turn on the television. Chances are you will see images of girls who don't look like you or your friends. This "perfect-bodied, pretty-faced" girl doesn't look like any of us. Body image is a very big problem with girls today.

The Just Think Foundation, which promotes media literacy in kids, is working on a body image project. Executive director Elana Yonah Rosen says the goal is for you to understand what the media is telling you about your body and be able to interpret its messages.

The percentage of girls who are "happy with the way I am" drops from 60% to 29% between elementary school and high school, according to a Foundation survey. So what happens to all those girls? First, Elana explains, girls believe they must look a certain way to attract boys (research shows that girls actually care about their appearance more than boys do). The advertising industry makes profits playing on your fears that you aren't tall enough, thin enough, or beautiful enough, so that you will buy products or clothes that it says will make you tall, thin, or beautiful. Elana says that beauty has been around throughout history, but that not being beautiful *enough* is a new creation of the advertising industry. Finally, some girls are affected by things their parents and other adults tell them, which may include what to eat, how to eat, and how to look. Elana thinks that some parents don't realize how important it is for them to support their girls and to be aware of the effects of their comments.

Elana points out that the popular, extreme fad diets are NOT healthy. When you diet, your body loses weight, but what it starts to lose first is muscle. Fat comes off last. When you start to diet, your metabolism slows down because your body says, "Oops, there's less food coming in, so we'd better slow down metabolizing that food or we may burn out of energy." When you start eating regularly again, your body takes longer to metabolize than it did before, so you gain weight more quickly than you did before you went on that diet! The other thing that happens after you've been on a diet is you retain more fat than you did before. So even if you are the same weight, you may end up with less muscle and more fat after you've dieted.

Girls who have fun playing sports or develop some athletic ability are healthier and have a stronger sense of themselves, and their self-esteem doesn't seem to fall into the typical decline around junior high. "There are not enough great sports role models for women," Elana says, "but those who exist are extremely important to promote so girls realize that yes, they too can be athletes and depend upon their bodies and minds in a way of strength rather than simple beauty." What your body can do is way more important than how it looks.

Did You Know?

Teenage girls who are more physically active in their spare time are much less likely to start smoking cigarettes, get involved with drugs, or become pregnant. Girls who play sports have a more positive body image. Half of all girls who participate in some kind of sports have higher-than-average levels of self-esteem and are less depressed.

Eating Issues

Recent studies show that over 40% of fifth- to eighth-grade girls want to lose weight and/or have dieted. When people try to lose too much weight or do it in a way that is unhealthy, they may develop an eating disorder. Two common eating disorders are anorexia, where a person starves herself, and bulimia, where a person eats too much (binges) and then makes herself vomit (purges). Eating disorders are very serious and can even cause death.

Eating disorders hurt athletes' performances by:

* making muscles tire and injure more easily

* decreasing coordination and good judgment

* stopping menstruation, causing the body to lose minerals that keep bones strong

Athletes sometimes feel even more pressure to be thin, because they think they have to look a certain way for competition or because they think it will make them better athletes.

An important resource, if you or a friend ever needs help, is: American Anorexia/Bulimia Association, 165 W. 46th Street, Suite 1108, New York, NY 10036; 212-575-6200.

HIGH PROFILE: CATHY RIGBY

Cathy Rigby earned the highest U.S. scores in gymnastics at the 1968 Olympics and led her team to fourth place at the 1972 Olympics (the highest ever for a U.S. team). During her career as a gymnast, Cathy developed an eating disorder because she thought she had to be thin to win in competition.

New Moon: How did you get started in gymnastics?

Cathy Rigby: I started when I was ten years old. Prior to that, I had about three years of ballet. I was very active as a young child, always climbing up on refrigerators, bookshelves, and things like that. One day, my older brother came home and he told me there was a trampoline at our local youth center. The first time I stepped into the gym and started jumping, I just fell in love with it.

NM: How old were you when you became aware that you had an eating disorder?

CR: When I was fifteen years old, I made my first Olympic team. I still had not reached puberty, and maintaining my weight was easy. At sixteen, though, I started puberty, including gaining some weight. And the very thing that gave me my identity, my self-worth, and my self-esteem — gymnastics — was being threatened by something that was very natural in my life — my weight. It really wasn't, but that's how I thought of it. I started restricting my diet. I started becoming bulimic, because I didn't know any other way of maintaining my weight.

NM: How did you overcome bulimia?

CR: I had an eating disorder for twelve years. I had to go through a lot of life changes. The first thing I really had to learn how to do was to communicate. That was difficult to do, because I had left that up to my coach to do for me. I also ended up getting professional help for my eating disorder.

NM: How can a young athlete deal with pressure from peers, coaches, or judges to be too thin?

CR: Coaches — and parents — are becoming more aware. Unfortunately, there are problems with the whole setup [of the sport]. You start a young girl at six or seven, and the only thing she learns is what goes on in the gym, especially if she's competing at top levels. So her whole identity comes from one source. There needs to be a balance. You need to have another life, of giving, of being involved in other people's lives. And you become a better competitor for it, because you're more willing to take a chance and go for it, and not be afraid.

NM: What would you say to a girl athlete who was worrying about her weight?

CR: I would tell her to make sure she has an understanding of nutrition and how it is important that she not starve herself or throw up everything she eats. Because in the end, it will weaken her, the results will not be what she wants, and it will be destructive to her career. Also, I would remind her that you are only in [competitive] sports ten or twelve years of your life. You also cannot feel that you are a failure if you do not win all the time. You have to understand that if you work at something and you are enjoying it — that's success!

—Kerri, age 13, Minnesota

CHAPTER FIVE

Fun with Sports

We know, we know: sports are already fun! But there are ways you can have even more fun and games in the sporting life. On the other hand, if P.E. and school teams have got you down by seeming too much like, well, schoolwork, here's a chance for you to reassociate sports with fun. Try any of the following ideas:

A Writing Workout

Keeping a sports journal is a great way to keep track of your progress as an athlete. What should you write down? Whatever you want. Examples are goals, times, and distances. What you write isn't as important as developing the daily habit of paying attention to your body health and fitness. A journal can make it easier to stay motivated when you feel stuck at a plateau with your goals. Reading it may give you hints about why you're having problems. For example, you may notice that you don't score as many points in your tennis match whenever you've had a sleepover the night before.

Take a Hike

Is it summer, and are you aching for a swim but have no way to get to the town pool? Why not hike to that river/stream/lake a mile or two from your house? Organize a party, whip up some healthy food, grab some water bottles and swimsuits, and call your friends. Or go on a solitary adventure (use common sense, though; safety first!). Not only will you get some exercise and have fun hiking, but a nice dip will be quite rewarding after your trudge in the heat. (Live in the suburbs or an urban area? Don't despair: a pool will seem just as good after your walk.)

Game Boys

Remember in fourth grade when you and your fellow girls took on the boys in a high-competition game of soccer and it was such a blast? Bring back that spirit of absolute, pure fun, and get together a boys-against-girls game in soccer, volleyball, field hockey, lacrosse, or whatever sport you adore. You still know the chant: "Girls Rule, Boys Drool, YAY!!!!!!!"

Sports Olympics

Organize your own Olympics. Get your friends and your friends' friends together for a day of sports. Have a baseball game, a basketball game, a soccer game, a dodge ball game, and whatever else you can think of.

Dedicate part of the day to making up your own games. Be prepared. Have lots of balls, bats, and everything else you can think of on hand. Be creative. If you don't have a basketball hoop, try making one out of things you find around the house. At the end of the day, give everyone a certificate of participation. Don't forget to have food and drinks on hand. Send everyone home with a page or two about women's history in sports. Do research about it on the Web and at the library, and interview your family. Who knows, you may have so much fun that you want to make your Olympics two or three days long!

If you feel too old for this, get all the little kids in your neighborhood together. Teach them about sportsmanship and how to play each game. You probably want to make it only an hour or two long; otherwise the kids will probably lose interest. The most important thing is to HAVE FUN!!!

Back to the Future

Did you ever play croquet? How about badminton? Lawn bowling? Invite a few of your pals to an old-fashioned garden party with the kinds of games girls would have played at the beginning of the twentieth century. Refreshments? Tea and cucumber sandwiches, of course!

Try Something New

There are tons of sports that aren't as popular in the U.S. as they are in other countries. Go to the library and ask for a book on international sports, and then get a group together to try playing one of them. Here are some ideas:

Cricket

Rugby

Bocce

Curling

Hold a Day at the Races

Have a traditional field day, complete with relay races, three-legged races, sack races, tug-of-war, balloon tossing, and obstacle courses. Find a big, grassy field at a school or park to hold your event. Be sure to have plenty of cold drinks for everyone. Hint: watermelon hits the spot perfectly.

Play with Parents

Sports are especially fun when it's kids playing against parents. That's what one girl's team did at the end of the soc-

Losing the Woman in Me

When I was young I was a tomboy
Because "Only boys were strong."
It was only now that I realized
That statement was totally wrong.
People say women are helpless
Always meek and mild,
Live life to only get married
Stay faithful and have a child.
When I was young I was angry
Because things like math and science
"Are not for little girls like you."
When I asked if I could play baseball
I was quickly turned away
Because sports like hockey and baseball
"Are not games that girls should play."
I was rejected because of my gender,
I was frightened but I could not win,
But then I was only a child
Did I have another choice but to give in?
But now that I am older I've realized
Just how strong I can be,
And I can do math and play baseball
Without losing the woman in me.

—Lara, age 16, Ontario

cer season. Her team was in shape for the game, but the parents seemed like they didn't even want to move from their positions. The parents would try to block, and the girls would just run right by. In the end, the score was 3–2: the girls' first win of the season! After the game was the most fun part: they all went out for pizza.

Invent a Sport

For a great group activity, create a new sport. You can base it on an existing sport or invent something totally new and off-the-wall. For example, you could decide to play soccer with the hands instead of the feet. Call it Hander, make a new set of rules, and you've got a new game. Or think of something no game has — like dribbling in the air instead of on the ground — and base your game on that. Be creative!

Quiz Yourself!

Get together a group of friends, or else try this yourself: see how many of the following fitness and sports terms you know. (Check the definitions, courtesy of the Women's Sports Foundation, on page 87.)

* aerobic exercise
* anaerobic exercise
* calisthenics
* cardiorespiratory fitness
* cardiovascular efficiency
* circuit training
* cool down
* endurance
* flexibility
* interval training
* main set

Sports Scavenger Hunt

Create a scavenger hunt with a sporty twist: to retrieve each item on the list, a player has to complete some physical task. For example, you might have people bike to the other side of town to get a napkin from your favorite pizza place, or find a way across a stream or pond to search for an object on the other side.

Orienteering

Whether it's just you and a friend or a whole gang of girls, orienteering is an unusual and exciting way to be outside. Choose a woody area that you'd like to explore, and find a map of it. If there are more than a few of you, it will be fun—and challenging—to split up into groups of two and

75

three. Supply each group with a map of the area and a compass, and set out from different spots to a predetermined destination. To orient yourself on the map, use your compass to determine which direction you're facing, and then turn the map until that direction is at the top. Then put your thumb on your location on the map. As you move around, trace your path with your thumb.

A few things to be careful about: make sure that the area you're exploring is safe and that your parents know where you are. Finish well before dark, and always stay with a buddy.

Around the World

If you're playing tennis with a lot of friends, you can try this game. Divide up and start all in a line on each side of the court. You hit the ball, run to the other side of the court, and get in line for your next hit. If you hit the ball into the net or it goes outside the court, you are out. The people who are out sit on the side. Once there are two people left, they have to run furiously to get to the ball on time. They run around the court in circles, until one of them hits the ball out or into the net and there is a winner.

Game Point Bang!

The tennis ball sails freely across the net, and back again.

Bang, Swish Bang, Swish Bang back and forth, eyes watching it,
fascinated.

THEN......it flies out.

One point for Brenda.

Now the battered ball retires and a new ball goes in. Swish

Bang, Swish Bang, Bang; the process continues.

OUT!......One point for Lynn.

Bang, Bang, Swish Bang, Swish Bang, Bang, Back, Forth, Back, Forth.

The crowd is hushed, it's GAMEPOINT.

Swish bang, swish bang, bang. That's the only noise you can hear.

Out!........................Who has won?

LYNN!

The crowd roars! Next Match. Bang, Swish Bang, Swish Bang, Bang.

—Morgan, age 12, Washington

H.O.R.S.E.

You can play H.O.R.S.E. as long as you have more than one person! You start at a point on one side of a basketball court and shoot from different spots, working your way around to the other side. You try to get the ball into the hoop. If you miss, you get the letter "H" and it's the next person's turn. If you don't miss, you move on to the next shooting point— and so on. The first one to spell H.O.R.S.E. loses.

CHAPTER SIX

Finding Out More About Sports

A comprehensive list of resources for the New Moon girl to keep exploring sports.

Books (Nonfiction)

All About Football, by George Sullivan (Putnam Publishing Group, 1990)

The All-American Girls Professional Baseball League (American Events), by Trudy J. Hanmer (New Discovery, 1994)

Babe Didrikson Zaharias: Champion Athlete (American Women of Achievement), by Elizabeth Lynn, R. Twombly, and Matina S. Horner (Chelsea House Publishers, 1989)

Basketball for Women: Becoming a Complete Player, by Nancy Lieberman-Cline, Robin Roberts, Kevin Warneke, and Pat Summit (Human Kinetics Publishers, 1995)

Big Girl in the Middle, by Gabrielle Reece and Karen Karbo (Three Rivers Press, 1998)

Coming On Strong: Gender and Sexuality in Twentieth-Century Women's Sport, by Susan K. Cahn (Belknap Press, 1994)

Crashing the Old Boys' Network: The Tragedies and Triumphs of Girls and Women in Sports, by David F. Salter (Praeger Publishers, 1996)

Girls Pro Baseball League, by Trudy J. Hanmer (Silver Burdett Press, 1994)

In These Girls, Hope Is a Muscle, by Madeleine Blais (Warner Books, 1996)

It's a Girl Thing: How to Stay Healthy, Safe, and in Charge, by Mavis Jukes (Knopf, 1997)

Karate for Kids, by J. Allen Queen (Sterling Publications, 1995)

Little Girls in Pretty Boxes: The Making and Breaking of Elite Gymnasts and Figure Skaters, by Joan Ryan (Warner Books, 1996)

Living the Dream, by Dot Richardson (Kensington Publishing Corp., 1998)

Self-Defense and Assault Prevention for Girls and Women, by Bruce Tegner (Thor Publishing Co., 1982)

Softball for Girls and Women, by Gladys C. Meyer (Macmillan General Reference, 1984)

Taking Charge of My Mind and Body, by Gladys Folkers, M.A., and Jeanne Engelmann (Free Spirit Publishers, 1997)

Up to the Plate: The All American Girls Baseball League (Sports Legacy), by Margot Fortunato Galt (Lerner Publications Co., 1995)

A Whole New Ball Game: The Story of the All-American Professional Baseball League, by Sue Macy (Henry Holt & Co., 1993)

Wilma Rudolph (American Women of Achievement), by Tom Biracree (All America Distributors Corp., 1990)

Winning Basketball for Girls, by Faye Young Miller and Wayne Coffey (Facts on File, 1992)

Winning Soccer for Girls, by Deborah Crisfield (Facts on File, 1996)

Winning Volleyball for Girls, by Deborah Crisfield (Facts on File, 1996)

Winning Ways: A Photo History of Women in Sports, by Sue Macy (Scholastic, 1998)

Books (Fiction)

Another Way to Dance, by Martha Southgate (Delacorte Press, 1996)

Basketball Girl of the Year, by Amelia Walden (out of print; 1970)

Girls in Love, by Cherie Bennett (Point, 1996)

Happily Ever After, by Anna Quindlen (Puffin, 1997)

In Lane Three, Alex Archer, by Tessa Duder (Bantam, 1991)

In the Year of the Boar and Jackie Robinson, by Bette Bao Lord (Harper Trophy, 1986)

Just for Kicks, by Paul Baczewski (out of print; 1990)

Never Say Quit, by Bill Wallace (Holiday House, 1993)

Run for Your Life, by Marilyn Levy (Houghton Mifflin, 1996)

Running Girl: The Diary of Ebonee Rose, by Sharon Bell Mathis (Harcourt Brace, 1997)

A Season of Comebacks, by Kathy Mackel (Putnam, 1997)

Skating Shoes, by Noel Streatfeild (out of print; 1964)

Tell Me If the Lovers Are Losers, by Cynthia Voigt (Fawcett, 1990)

There's a Girl in My Hammerlock, by Jerry Spinelli (Aladdin Paperbacks,1993)

Internet

www.newmoon.org
The inside scoop on *New Moon*, with stories from the magazine, contests, and other fun interactive features.

www.bennygoodsport.com
A fitness Web site designed to help kids have fun and learn how to be healthy.

www.bicycleguide.com
This popular site provides bicycle news and product information.

www.caaws.ca
The Canadian Association for the Advancement of Women and Sport and Physical Activity Web site is designed to get girls off the sidelines and onto the field.

www.cnnsi.com/siforwomen
Sports Illustrated for Women online.

www.freshandtasty.com
This online women's snowboarding magazine features interviews and Web links for female snowboarders.

www.getrolling.com
This inline skating mag has tips about inline skating as well as a bookstore and skating links.

www.gogirlmag.com
An empowering sports and fitness magazine for women and girls.

www.gsusa.org
The site introducing you to the Girl Scouts of the U.S.A., which now has a sports program.

www.ifba.com
The official site of the International Female Boxers Association offers rankings, schedules, merchandise, and more.

www.justwomen.com
Just SPORTS for Women has news and chat about women in sports.

www.lifetimetv.com/sports
This site hosted by Lifetime television for women has information about the WNBA; it's also the site for the Women's Sports Foundation.

www.majorleaguebaseball.com/women
The official site of Major League Baseball has historical and current information about women and girls in baseball.

www.melpomene.org
A fun and interesting site all about girls' health, sports, and other physical activities.

www.nike.com/girls
The Girls in the Game site has important information like tips and sporting advice, as well as profiles of and articles by teen athletes around the country.

www.runnersworld.com
This leading site for runners of all ages provides advice, current information, and news about running.

www.shegear.com
Provides equipment and adventure for women.

www.surfergrrl.com
Surfer Girl is the online version of the print magazine, providing information and fun articles for female surfers.

www.troom.com/sportsandfitness
The Tampax site has an area devoted to sports and fitness, which links to other girls' sports sites.

www.wggn.com
Women's Gateway Golf Network offers historical information, tournament dates, and event information for women golfers.

www.wnba.com
The official site of the women's basketball league has tons of game and player information for fans of the WNBA.

www.wombats.org
The Woman's Mountain Bike and Tea Society site offers riding tips, "batty art," events, and stories about women mountain bikers around the country.

www.womensmultisport.com
This site features interviews, event information, and tips for many different women's sports.

www.womensoccer.com
This site is dedicated to worldwide coverage of women's soccer and provides commentary, team schedules, and more.

Organizations

AAU/USA Youth Sports Program
3400 W. 86th Street
Indianapolis, IN 46268
800-AAU-4USA (800-228-4872)

American Sport Education Program
P.O. Box 5076
Champaign, IL 61825-5076
217-351-5076 fax: 217-351-2674

National Association for Girls and Women in Sport
1900 Association Drive
Reston, VA 20191
703-476-3450

National Youth Sports Program/ Collegiate Athletic Association
6201 College Boulevard
Overland Park, KS 66211
913-339-1906 fax: 913-339-0028

U.S. Olympic Committee Disabled Sports Services
One Olympic Plaza
Colorado Springs, CO 80909-5760
719-578-4818 fax: 719-578-4976
e-mail: mark.shepherd@usoc.org

Women's Sports Foundation
Eisenhower Park
East Meadow, NY 11554
800-227-3988

YMCA Youth Sports
37 W. Broad Street, Suite 600
Columbus, OH 43215
614-621-1231 fax: 614-224-5611

Junior Olympic Archery Development
One Olympic Plaza
Colorado Springs, CO 80909-5778
719-578-4576 fax: 719-632-4733

Youth Basketball of America, Inc.
10325 Orangewood Blvd.
Orlando, FL 32821
407-363-YBOA (363-9262)

American Bicycle Association
1645 West Sunrise Blvd.
Gilbert, AZ 85233
602-961-1903 fax: 602-961-1842

National Bicycle League
3958 Brown Park Drive, Suite D
Hilliard, OH 43026
614-777-1625 fax: 614-777-1680

U.S. Junior Regional Cycling Program
One Olympic Plaza
Colorado Springs, CO 80909
719-578-4845 fax: 719-578-4628

American Junior Golf Association
2415 Steeplechase Lane
Roswell, GA 30076
770-998-4653
e-mail: ALGA@aol.com

USA Gymnastics
201 S. Capitol Avenue, Suite 300
Indianapolis, IN 46225
317-237-5050 fax: 317-237-5069

U.S. Dressage Federation, Inc.
7700 A Street
Lincoln, NE 68510
402-434-8550 fax: 402-434-8570

United States Pony Clubs, Inc.
4071 Iron Works Pike
Lexington, KY 40511
606-254-7669 fax: 606-233-4652

United States Figure Skating Association
20 First Street
Colorado Springs, CO 80906
719-635-5200 fax: 719-635-9548
e-mail: USFAl@aol.com

United States Amateur Confederation of Roller Skating
P.O. Box 6579
Lincoln, NE 68506
402-483-7551 fax: 402-483-1465
e-mail: SK*SID@aol.com

U.S. International Speedskating Association
P.O. Box 16157
Rocky River, OH 44116
440-899-0128 fax: 440-899-0109

U.S. Skiing and Snowboarding Association
1500 Kearns Boulevard, Building F
P.O. Box 100
Park City, UT 84060
801-649-9090 fax: 801-649-3613

United States Youth Soccer Association
899 Presidential Drive, Suite 117
Richardson, TX 75081
800-4-SOCCER (800-476-2237)

Amateur Softball Association
2801 N.E. 50th Street
Oklahoma City, OK 73111
405-424-5266 fax: 405-424-3855

Babe Ruth League
1770 Brunswick Pike
Trenton, NJ 08638
609-695-1434 fax: 317-630-1369

Cinderella Softball Leagues
P.O. Box 1411
Corning, NY 14830
607-937-5469

PONY Baseball and Softball
300 Clare Drive
Washington, PA 15301
724-225-1060 fax: 412-225-9852

National Scholastic Surfing Association
P.O. Box 495
Huntington Beach, CA 92648
714-536-0445 fax: 714-960-4380

United States Swimming, Inc.
One Olympic Plaza
Colorado Springs, CO 80909
719-578-4578 fax: 719-578-4669

United States Taekwondo Union, Inc.
One Olympic Plaza
Colorado Springs, CO 80909
719-578-4632 fax: 719-578-4642

National Junior Tennis League
70 W. Red Oak Lane
White Plains, NY 10604
914-696-7000 fax: 914-696-7167

U.S.A. Track and Field
P.O. Box 120
Indianapolis, IN 46206-0120
317-261-0500 fax: 317-261-0481

U.S.A. Junior Olympic Volleyball
3595 E. Fountain Boulevard, Suite I-2
Colorado Springs, CO 80910
719-637-8300 fax: 719-597-6307
e-mail: jkessel@usa-volleyball.org

ANSWERS TO QUIZ ON PAGES 74–75

Aerobic exercise: rhythmical exercise that causes an increase in heart rate and is done for an amount of time requiring an increased intake of oxygen. Running is aerobic.

Anaerobic exercise: quick, short-term, high-intensity movements requiring no increase in oxygen intake. Weightlifting is anaerobic.

Calisthenics: exercises performed for the purpose of muscular development and/or flexibility, without implements.

Cardiorespiratory fitness: the heart's ability to pump blood and deliver oxygen throughout your body.

Cardiovascular efficiency: the most important component of physical fitness: the capacity of your heart and lungs to function efficiently so oxygen is brought to the tissue and waste products are removed from the body.

Circuit training: sequence of exercise activities performed at individual stations within a time limit.

Cool down: movements that help the body to slow down, stretch out, and relax after rigorous exercise; also help the heart rate to return to its normal, resting rate.

Endurance: the quality that allows muscles to exert repeatedly with a force or static contraction over a period of time.

Flexibility: range of motion of a specific joint and its corresponding muscle group.

Interval training: the repetitions of an exercise performed at an intensity above that of anaerobic activity, alternated with a period of rest or light exercise.

Main set: the central part of your workout; the times vary from 20 to 60 minutes for a workout, and one of the main goals is to reach a target heart rate.

Hi! My name is *Flynn Berry*. I'm 11 years old and live in a barely there, tiny teeny little speck-on-the-map suburb of New York City, New York. I love to write and create any form of art (collages, paintings, drawings, etc.). I am also interested in helping humans, including myself, stop hurting animals; playing soccer; karate; playing the flute; reading (particularly any Philip Pullman books, and anything by Madeleine L'Engle); exploring New York City; and spending time with my friends.

My name is *Lauren Noelani Calhoun,* and I am 13 years old. I live on the island of Kauai, Hawaii. I enjoy cooking, playing the oboe, hiking and camping, dancing, running, and spending time with friends. I have a service club called the Kids Helping Kids Club and volunteer at a women's shelter. I baby-sit whenever I get a chance, and I am learning to cook with a chef in a local restaurant. I hope to be a chef when I grow up, but we'll see!

My name is *Ashley Cofell*. I live in a small town in Minnesota. I'm 10 years old. I started writing books when I was seven or eight. I have written four books, which I have given to friends and family. I like to read short stories, especially scary ones. I also like to play soccer, swim, cook, ride my bike, go to the theater, and sing. I've been in two choirs. I want to be a writer and a doctor when I grow up.

My name is *Morgan Fykes*. I'm 12 years old, and I live in a large old house with a big porch and a room of my own in Washington, D.C. I'm in sixth grade at a private school for girls. I'm cheerful and I talk a lot, except when I'm meeting new people. My mom and I started a mother-daughter book club three years ago, and we wrote a book about the club. It was published last year, and I went on a book tour and did presentations on my own. I have an art section set up in one corner of my basement, and I also like dancing (tap, ballet, and jazz), sports, and camping.

My name is *Katie Hedberg*. I have a younger sister named Mollie and a younger brother named Sam. I also have an older half-brother named Daniel. I'm 11 years old and in sixth grade in Minnesota. I like to go shopping, hang with my friends, listen to CDs, read magazines, and do stuff that a normal 11-year-old would do. I play the piano and the trumpet and sing in choir. I had a chapter in the book *Girls Know Best*. I'm a Girl Scout and I help with my younger sister's troop.

My name is **Elizabeth Larsson** and I live near Philadelphia. Among many things, one of my passions is dancing. I love to dance, especially ballet. When I grow up, I probably want to go into the profession of sports medicine for dancers, or physical therapy. Other things I like to do are read, write, play on the computer, and anything that involves making something. I have my own business making silk eye pillows, filled with little seeds, to help you relax. My favorite foods are pizza, baked ziti, and chocolate. I go to an all-girls school, and I'm Quaker. I'm in the seventh grade.

I'm **Priscilla Mendoza**. I like listening to music, being outdoors, traveling, and trying new things. Soccer, gymnastics, and basketball are some of my favorite sports. My favorite color is lavender. On rainy days I like to grab a couple of friends and veg out on the couch to a couple of comedy or horror flicks. I'm 12 and in the seventh grade. I live in a college town in northern California. Someday I hope to be a journalist, a lawyer, or the president of my very own company...who knows? (But for now I'll stick to baby-sitting.)

Julia Peters-Axtell is from a small city in Minnesota. I used to be on the *New Moon* magazine board but decided to try something new, like this! I'm in eighth grade at a public high school. I have a little sister — Emma — and my two parents, who I love to death. My favorite things are: my parents, guys, my sister, gum, my friends, my cats, music, cappuccino, and dances. I love all kinds of sports, but especially I enjoy soccer, track, and softball. I am on the JV soccer and track teams.

My name is **Caitlin Stern** and I live in a small town in Alaska. I unschool, which means that I choose what I learn and how I learn it. I've played the piano since I was five (I'm 13 now), and the recorder since I was eight. I'm also learning Japanese. I like jogging, biking, ice skating, and downhill skiing. I like to read books by Philip Pullman, Jules Verne, and Daniel Quinn. I listen to rock mostly, especially the Beatles and Sean Lennon. I'm a Libra. I love hanging out with my friends, but most of them don't live in Alaska. I have lived in a lot of different places, like New Zealand, Bali, Hawaii, and England.

Celebrate and empower girls and women with New Moon Publishing!

"New Moon Publishing has an agenda for girls and young women that's refreshingly different from mainstream corporate media. New Moon is building a community of girls and young women intent on saving their true selves. New Moon's magazines are a godsend for girls and young women, for their parents and the adults who care about them."

—**Mary Pipher, Ph.D.,** author of *Reviving Ophelia: Saving the Selves of Adolescent Girls*

New Moon: The Magazine for Girls and Their Dreams
Edited by girls ages 8–14, *New Moon* is an ad-free international bimonthly magazine that is a joy to read at any age!

New Moon Network: For Adults Who Care About Girls
Share the successes and strategies of a worldwide network of parents, teachers, and other adults committed to raising healthy, confident girls.

Between the Moon and You
A catalog of delightful gifts that celebrate and educate girls and women. Visit at www.newmoooncatalog.com.

New Moon Education Division
A variety of interactive workshops and compelling speakers for conferences or conventions.

For information on any of these New Moon resources, contact:

New Moon Publishing
P.O. Box 3620
Duluth, MN 55803-3620
Toll-free: 800-381-4743 • Fax: 218-728-0314
E-mail: newmoon@newmoon.org
Web site: www.newmoon.org